# LITTLE MISS SCATTERBRAIN
## Causes Chaos

Roger Hargreaves

**MR. MEN**    **LITTLE MISS**

MR. MEN™ LITTLE MISS™ © THOIP (a Sanrio company)

Little Miss Scatterbrain Causes Chaos © 2014 THOIP (a Sanrio company)
Printed and published under licence from Price Stern Sloan, Inc., Los Angeles.
First published in France 1998 by Hachette Livre
This edition published in 2015 by Dean, an imprint of Egmont UK Limited,
The Yellow Building, 1 Nicholas Road, London W11 4AN

ISBN 978 0 6035 7130 5
61267/1
Printed in Great Britain

## EGMONT

Little Miss Scatterbrain was always forgetting things.

Whenever she met Mr Small she would call out, "What a fine day, Mr Tall."

Can you believe it! She really was a scatterbrain!

On this particular day, Little Miss Scatterbrain went to the grocers.

"Three onions, five tomatoes and two big carrots, please," she said.

"Are you making a soup?" asked the shopkeeper.

"Not at all," replied Little Miss Scatterbrain, surprised. "I'm making a fruit salad for my birthday!"

And off she went with her vegetables! What a scatterbrain!

And you'll never guess what she did next!

She got into Mr Topsy Turvy's car by mistake and drove off!

"Car!" he shouted. "Someone's stolen my thief!"

As usual he had got his words the wrong way round. Or was it the right way wrong?

And you won't be surprised to know that Mr Topsy Turvey's car could only drive backwards! Little Miss Scatterbrain was even more confused than usual! She stopped to ask a cow the way home.

Mooo! replied the cow.

How very scatterbrained to ask a cow the way home!

Mr Topsy Turvy went straight to the police station.

"A car," he explained, "has taken my thief!
You mustn't help me."

It took the poor policeman a long time to work out
what Mr Topsy Turvy was trying to say!

On the other side of the town, Mr Jelly was having a very bad day. He'd heard a strange noise coming from downstairs and, as you can imagine, this made him very nervous. In fact, he was hiding under his bed, shaking like a jelly.

"Home at last," said Little Miss Scatterbrain.
"But how odd. I was sure my kitchen was green.
Never mind, I must get cooking."

In the meantime, trembling and shaking like a leaf. Mr Jelly had made his way downstairs to find out what the noise was.

Imagine his shock when he saw a strange figure in his kitchen. A figure with a large, sharp knife!

"H … h … help m … m … me," he stammered, calling the police. "Burglars! Bandits! Pirates! Oh calamity!"

"Do not fear, Mr Jelly. We're on our way," said the policeman.

"You'd better come with me, Mr Topsy Turvy," said the policeman. "This terrible crime might have something to do with your missing car."

With sirens blaring, Mr Topsy Turvy and the policeman arrived at Mr Jelly's house.

"My cat! I mean my carpet! I mean my ..." exclaimed Mr Topsy Turvy.

"Car, sir?" said the policeman, helpfully.

"Pssst. The p … p … pirates are in the kitchen!" whispered Mr Jelly to the policeman.

"Leave this to me," replied the policeman.

"Happy birthday to me, happy birthday to me," sang Little Miss Scatterbrain to herself in the kitchen.

The policeman couldn't believe his eyes!

"Pirates indeed," he said smiling. "I should have known that you would have something to do with this muddle! And even less of a surprise as it's the first of April. April Fool's Day!"

"The first of April?" said Little Miss Scatterbrain, very much surprised. "Then it's not my birthday after all. My birthday is in July … I think," she added. "Silly me, but do join me for some fruit salad."

Onions, tomatoes and carrots … with sugar!

The policeman wasn't sure he liked this type of fruit salad. Mr Topsy Turvy didn't notice how strange it was, because he'd put his bowl under his hat!

"I must be going," said Little Miss Scatterbrain to her friends. "Thank you so much for coming, Mr Right Way and Mr Fireman."

And off she drove …

... in the police car!